For Piet & Putty

Library of Congress Cataloging-in-Publication Data

Quakenbush, Robert M.
  Sherlock Chick and the peekaboo mystery.

  Summary: In search of a missing baby mouse, Sherlock
Chick tries to imagine how a lost mouse would look for
his house.
  1. Mystery and detective stories. 2. Chickens—
Fiction. 3. Animals—Fiction. I. Title.
PZ7.Q16Sjy 1987   [E]   87-3591
ISBN 0-8193-1149-9

A Parents Magazine
Read Aloud Original

SHERLOCK CHICK AND THE PEEKABOO MYSTERY

by Robert Quackenbush

PARENTS MAGAZINE PRESS · NEW YORK

Mother Mouse came running
to Sherlock Chick.
"Help! Help!" she cried.
"I need a detective!
My child is lost!"
"I will take the case,"
said Sherlock Chick.
"Tell me the facts."

"My child's name is Squeakins,"
said Mother Mouse.
"I took him outside for the
first time this morning.
A cat came along and scared us.
I ran one way and my little
Squeakins ran another.
That is how I lost him."

"Show me his picture,"
said Sherlock Chick.
Mother Mouse took him
to her house.
She showed Sherlock Chick
a picture of Squeakins.
"Where could he be?"
she pleaded.

Sherlock Chick said, "You
told me that he had never been
away from home before.
So he must be looking for
a house like his own house."
"But I don't know of any other
mouse houses around here,"
said Mother Mouse.
"Leave it to me," said
Sherlock Chick.

Sherlock Chick went outside.
"How will I know a mouse house
when I see one?" he wondered.
He looked at the door to
Mother Mouse's house.
"I know," he said. "It will
have a hole for a doorway."
He went on his way.

Sherlock Chick came to a tree.
He saw a hole.
He saw two eyes watching
from inside the hole.
"Peek-a-boo! I see you!"
said Sherlock Chick.
"Are you a little mouse
hiding in there?"
Out came...

...a raccoon!
"No mouse here,"
said the raccoon.
"Sorry," said Sherlock Chick.
"I came to the wrong house."
He went on his way.

Sherlock Chick came to a hill.
He saw a hole.
He saw two eyes watching
from inside the hole.
"Peek-a-boo! I see you!"
said Sherlock Chick.
"Are you a little mouse
hiding in there?"
Out came...

...a rabbit!
"No mouse here,"
said the rabbit.
"Sorry," said Sherlock Chick.
"I came to the wrong house."
He went on his way.

Sherlock Chick came to a bush.
He saw a hole.
He saw two eyes watching
from inside the hole.
"Peek-a-boo! I see you!"
said Sherlock Chick.
"Are you a little mouse
hiding in there?"
Out came...

...a baby fox!
"No mouse here,"
said the fox.
"Sorry," said Sherlock Chick.
"I came to the wrong house."
He went on his way.

Sherlock Chick came to a basket.
He saw a hole.
He saw two eyes watching
from inside the hole.
"Peek-a-boo! I see you!"
said Sherlock Chick.
"Are you a little mouse
hiding in there?"
Out came...

...a cat!

"Did you say mouse?"
said the cat. "Where?
I saw two this morning.
But they ran away."

"Sorry," said Sherlock Chick.
"I came to the wrong house."
He went on his way.

Sherlock Chick came to a
tiny wooden house.
He saw a hole for a doorway
and two eyes watching.
"Peek-a-boo! I see you!"
said Sherlock Chick.
"Are you a little mouse
hiding in there?"
Out came...

...a puppy!
"No mouse here,"
said the puppy.
"Sorry," said Sherlock Chick.
"I came to the wrong house."
He went on his way.

Sherlock Chick came
to a drainpipe.
He saw two eyes
watching from
inside the pipe.
"Peek-a-boo! I see you!"
said Sherlock Chick.
"Are you a little mouse
hiding in there?"
Out came...

...a little mouse!
"Yes!" cried the mouse.
"And I am lost!"
Sherlock Chick looked at
the picture of Squeakins.
Then he looked at the mouse.
"Indeed you are," he said.
"And I know whose little
mouse you are.
Come, I'll take you home."

Together they ran
past the puppy's house,
past the cat's house,
past the baby fox's house,
past the rabbit's house,
past the raccoon's house...

...all the way home
to Mother Mouse!

"The case is solved,"
said Sherlock Chick happily.

About the Author

Sherlock Chick and the Peekaboo Mystery,
the second book in the popular new mystery
series, was inspired by a kitten Robert
Quackenbush bought for his son, Piet. Like
the animals in this story, the kitten loves to
hide. So whenever the Quackenbush family
can't find their furry friend, they know to
look for two mischievous eyes peering out of
a dark closet or cabinet.

Robert Quackenbush has illustrated
nearly 150 children's books, over half of
which he has also written; he created the
popular *Henry the Duck* series for Parents.
He has received many honors for his work,
including an Edgar Allen Poe Special Award
for best children's mystery. In addition to
creating picture books, Mr. Quackenbush
owns an art gallery in New York City,
where he teaches painting, writing,
and illustrating.